DAVID LUCAS

The Robot and the Bluebird

ANDERSEN PRESS LONDON

There once was a Robot
with a *broken* heart.

to Yoko

with special thanks to
Janice Thomson

other books by David Lucas:
Halibut Jackson
Nutmeg
Whale

First published in Great Britain in 2007 by Andersen Press Ltd., 20 Vauxhall Bridge Road, London SW1V 2SA.
Published in Australia by Random House Australia Pty., Level 3, 100 Pacific Highway, North Sydney, NSW 2060.
Copyright © David Lucas, 2007. The rights of David Lucas to be identified as the author and illustrator
of this work have been asserted by him in accordance with the Copyright, Designs and Patents Act, 1988.
All rights reserved.
Colour separated in Switzerland by Photolitho AG, Zürich.
Printed and bound by Tien Wah Press, Singapore.

10 9 8 7 6 5 4 3 2 1

British Library Cataloguing in Publication Data available.

ISBN 978 1 84270 623 7

They did their best to fix him,
but it wasn't any good.

So he was sent to sit on the scrapheap,
with all the other old machines.

He tried talking to them –
he said, "My heart was broken, you know,"
but they didn't answer.

So he lay down and looked up at the sky.
He lay there through the long, dark nights and the empty days.

He lay there rusting in the Autumn rain.
He lay there when the first snows of Winter fell.

And there, one day, was a Bluebird, fighting against the freezing wind.
She landed on his shoulder.

"What are you doing here, little bird?" he said.
"I'm flying south," she said weakly, "south, where the sun shines.
But I'm so cold and tired I can go no further."
"I'm sure you don't want to stay here," said the Robot, "I'm rubbish."
But the Bluebird just shivered and said nothing.

"There's a space where my heart used to be,"
he said gently. "You can sleep there if you like."

So the Bluebird settled down to sleep,
on a nest the Robot made.

And as the Robot looked out into the night,
he was astonished to feel as if he had a warm, living, beating heart.
And when the Bluebird fluttered,
he felt as if his own heart were fluttering.

The next morning, the door to his heart opened
and the Bluebird sang, sweet and bright in the icy air.

"My old heart only ever said *tick tock*," said the Robot,
"but now my heart is *singing*."

And the Bluebird flew a little way up into the air,
and the Robot felt like his heart was *flying*.
And creaking, he got to his feet,
and danced a creaking, clanking dance.

"I wish I could live in your heart,"
said the Bluebird,
"but I'll die of cold if I stay here.
Winter has come so soon
and I still have so far to go.
I don't even know if I have the strength,"
she said sadly,
settling in his hand.

"Then let me carry you," said the Robot.
"I'll carry you in my heart,
and shelter you from the cold and storms."

And so he carried her in his heart,
across frozen wastes,
over towering mountains,
through blizzards and fog,
though now he was deathly tired
and his joints groaned with every step.

And when at last the Sun shone,
he opened the door to his heart
and out flew the Bluebird,
singing and twittering 'thank you's.

The Robot lifted his arms toward her,
but he couldn't take another step.
His strength had failed at last.
"Make your home in my heart,"
he said, in the faintest whisper,
and he hung his head.

And the Bluebird lived in his heart *always*.

And the Robot stands there still,
his arms outstretched,
like an old, hollow tree,
home every year
to singing birds.